The Best Gift of All

Written by Cornelis Wilkeshuis
Illustrated by Rita van Bilsen

St. Paul Books & Media

Library of Congress Cataloging-in-Publication Data

Wilkeshuis, C.
[Das schönste geschenk. English]
The best gift of all / written by Cornelis Wilkeshuis :
illustrated by Rita van Bilsen.
p. cm.
Translation from the German version of: Das schönste geschenk .
ISBN 0-8198-1126-2
1. Jesus Christ—Fiction. [1. Jesus Christ—Nativity—Fiction.
2. Christmas—Fiction.] I. Bilsen, Rita van. ill. II. Title.
PZ7.W648395Be 1989 89-38122
[E]—dc20 CIP
AC

Published and printed in the U.S.A. by St. Paul Books & Media
50 St. Paul's Ave., Boston, MA 02130

St. Paul Books & Media is the publishing house of the Daughters of St. Paul, an international congregation of women religious serving the Church with the communications media.

1 2 3 4 5 6 7 8 9 97 96 95 94 93 92 91 90 89

For Véronique and Xenia

Balthasar was a kind and friendly man. He was also one of the smartest kings who had ever reigned in his country. A wise teacher had long ago taught Balthasar how to study and read the stars.

Every evening, King Balthasar climbed to the top of the highest tower of his castle to look at the stars. They sparkled and glittered like silver letters on dark velvet. They told him about things yet to be...happy days, good harvests, wars and floods.

One night Balthasar saw a star he had never seen before. It glowed so brightly that all the other stars looked like tiny sparks! The king looked at the star for a long time. Then he hurried to his library and found the book his wise, old teacher had left him. Balthasar read: "A star will appear in the east, and it will be bigger and brighter than any star ever seen before. Then, a Prince will be born who will reign over heaven and earth. He will bring peace to all people."

"I must find this Prince," thought Balthasar excitedly. "I, too, love peace. I don't like fighting and quarreling. Maybe I can help him make peace in the world."

The king put on his favorite cloak and crown and hurried to his court. He ordered the servants to get camels and horses ready for a long trip.

"Where are you going?" the people asked.

"We are going to follow the new star," said Balthasar. "We shall go wherever it leads us."

Early the next morning, while the stars were still out, the king and his soldiers got up. They saddled their horses and loaded their sleepy camels with food and water for the journey.

All the noise awoke the young prince, Irenus.

He ran down the stairs and across the courtyard. "Father, Father, where are you going?"

"I am taking this golden goblet to the new-born Prince of Peace."

"Where does the Prince live?" questioned Irenus.

"I don't know. Do you see that bright new star? It is his star. It will show us the way. We are going to follow it until we find the Prince."

"Can I go with you?" pleaded Irenus.

"No," said Balthasar. "The journey may be very long, and we will have to cross the great desert. Such a journey is not for children. Now go back to your room and go to sleep, Irenus." With that the king hugged his son and mounted his horse. The caravan began to move.

Irenus could hear the shrill flutes of the camel drivers and the deep singing of the soldiers long after they were gone from sight.

Irenus went back to his room. "I will follow the star and see the new Prince, too," he decided. "Father is bringing a golden goblet as a gift for the Prince. I will bring my three most favorite toys."

That evening Irenus packed the red bouncing ball his best friend had given him.

"It shines just like the golden goblet," he thought.

Next, he picked out his favorite book. The one his grandmother had made for him. She had drawn pictures of butterflies and birds, wild horses and camels, and had written

a verse under each picture. Then Irenus called his little white dog, Pluton, and put his leash on. His father had given him Pluton for his birthday, and Irenus was not really sure if he could ever give up his pet. Irenus thought Pluton was the most beautiful and intelligent dog in the whole kingdom.

Irenus walked and walked all night long, following the star carefully. Just as the sun was coming up, he reached a small village.

He found a shady spot under some palm trees and lay down to rest. When he woke up, he heard someone crying. "Why are you crying?" he asked a young girl.

"My clothes are torn and patched, and the other children laugh at me. No one will play with me," she sobbed.

"Oh, don't cry," said Irenus. "Please, take this ball. If you play with it, it will always play with you! It jumps high off the ground and into the air, and then it comes back to you. Now you will always have something to play with."

The little girl could hardly believe that the bouncing ball was hers to keep.

Evening came and the star shone brightly once more. Irenus continued on his way.

The next morning he came to a small house. An old man was sitting in front, rocking and sighing quite loudly.

"What's the matter, sir?" Irenus asked.

"I am old and sick," the man replied. "I used to travel all over the kingdom, even to foreign countries. Now I can't even walk to the next house. I am very lonely."

Irenus looked at his book with the beautiful pictures. "Here, take this. It is yours," he said, holding the book out to the old man. "This book has pictures of animals and flowers from all over the world."

The old man carefully opened the book and turned the pages. "How beautiful!" he exclaimed. "And there are verses, too. They will talk to me, and I won't be lonely any more."

The third night seemed longer than ever to Irenus. His feet hurt, and Pluton was panting. But the star shone brighter and brighter.

The next morning, Irenus found a farmhouse where he could rest. A small boy lived there who had injured his leg and could not walk. When he saw how Irenus could walk and run, he closed his mouth tight, turned his head toward the wall and said nothing more.

Irenus tried to talk to the boy, but he got no answer.

Pluton began to jump and play. Suddenly, the small dog jumped onto the bed and tickled the boy's face with his sloppy tongue and tiny paws until the boy began to laugh.

Irenus knew what he must do. Putting the end of Pluton's leash into the boy's hand, he quickly left the room and closed the door behind him.

Irenus stepped out into the night and felt hot tears starting down his cheeks. Oh, how he would miss his little playmate! He looked up at the star and began to run. He ran and ran until he stumbled and fell.

Irenus was so tired that he just lay there and went to sleep.

Irenus slept all day. When he finally woke up, he felt good inside and was happy to think of Pluton playing with the crippled boy.

As night fell, the star seemed as bright as the sun. It was shining right over a village. Irenus could see the rays of golden light beaming over a house on the hillside. He walked steadily toward the house and did not even notice his father's soldiers standing outside.

Inside the house a man and a woman were kneeling next to a cradle. And there, snuggled in the blankets, Irenus saw the new-born Prince of Peace.

Two other kings were standing with his father. One king was giving the baby a valuable vase, filled with precious myrrh. The other king gave a silver bowl full of incense. And Balthasar proudly presented the golden goblet.

Irenus bowed to the baby and turned toward the mother. He wanted to tell her about the lonely little girl to whom he had given his ball. And the old man to whom he had given his picture book. And the sad bed-ridden boy to whom he had given his playful dog. And now he had nothing left to give the Prince of Peace.

But the gentle woman seemed to understand. She smiled at Irenus, took his empty hands into hers and kissed them.

TO THINK AND TALK ABOUT

Irenus wanted to bring his three most treasured toys to the new-born Prince of Peace. But along the way he gave each of the toys to someone else.

Why did he give his ball to the little girl? And his book to the old man? And his dog to the crippled boy?

Do you think that Irenus made them happy?

Do you think that Irenus showed that he cared about them?

Did he have a gift to offer the Prince of Peace?

What was the gift Irenus gave to Jesus?

Why was it the best gift of all?